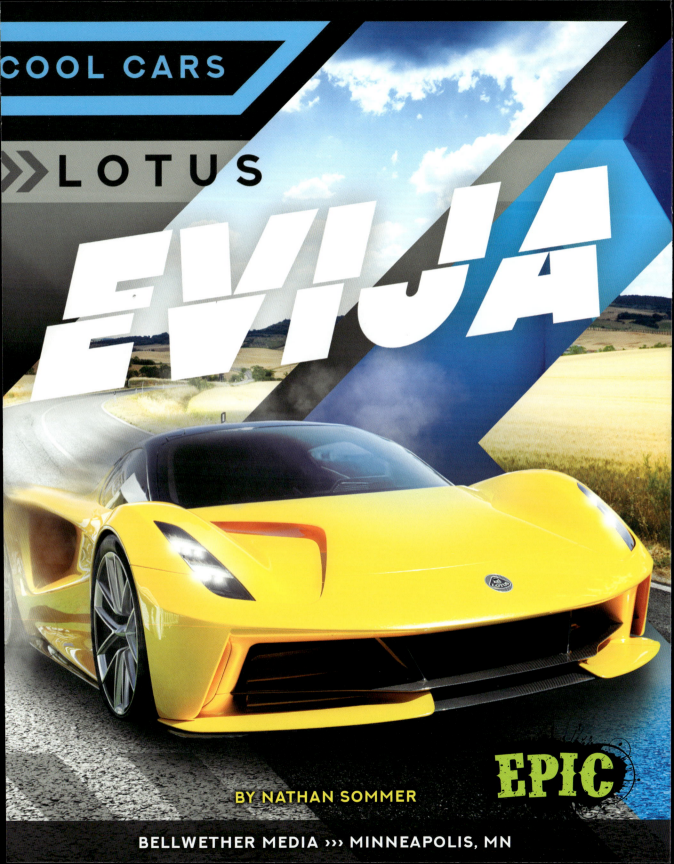

COOL CARS

LOTUS

EVIJA

BY NATHAN SOMMER

BELLWETHER MEDIA ››› MINNEAPOLIS, MN

EPIC

EPIC BOOKS are no ordinary books. They burst with intense action, high-speed heroics, and shadows of the unknown. Are you ready for an Epic adventure?

This edition first published in 2023 by Bellwether Media, Inc.

No part of this publication may be reproduced in whole or in part without written permission of the publisher. For information regarding permission, write to Bellwether Media, Inc., Attention: Permissions Department, 6012 Blue Circle Drive, Minnetonka, MN 55343.

Library of Congress Cataloging-in-Publication Data

LC record for Lotus Evija available at: https://lccn.loc.gov/2022020234

Text copyright © 2023 by Bellwether Media, Inc. EPIC and associated logos are trademarks and/or registered trademarks of Bellwether Media, Inc.

Editor: Kieran Downs   Designer: Jeffrey Kollock

Printed in the United States of America, North Mankato, MN

TABLE OF CONTENTS

A RARE RIDE	4
ALL ABOUT THE EVIJA	6
PARTS OF THE EVIJA	12
THE EVIJA'S FUTURE	20
GLOSSARY	22
TO LEARN MORE	23
INDEX	24

A RARE RIDE »

CHARGING STATION

A driver unplugs his Lotus Evija from the **charging station**. He gets in the car. Then he speeds off.

The car zooms around curves. The Evija is one powerful **electric car**!

ALL ABOUT THE EVIJA

THE LOTUS TRADITION

Most cars produced by Lotus begin with the letter E. This trend started in 1956.

LOTUS 18 IN 1961

Lotus began in Hethel, England, in 1952. The company started out by building race cars.

Lotus cars are **rare**. They are also expensive. Famous **models** include the Elan, Elise, and Evora.

EVORA

📍 WHERE IS IT MADE?

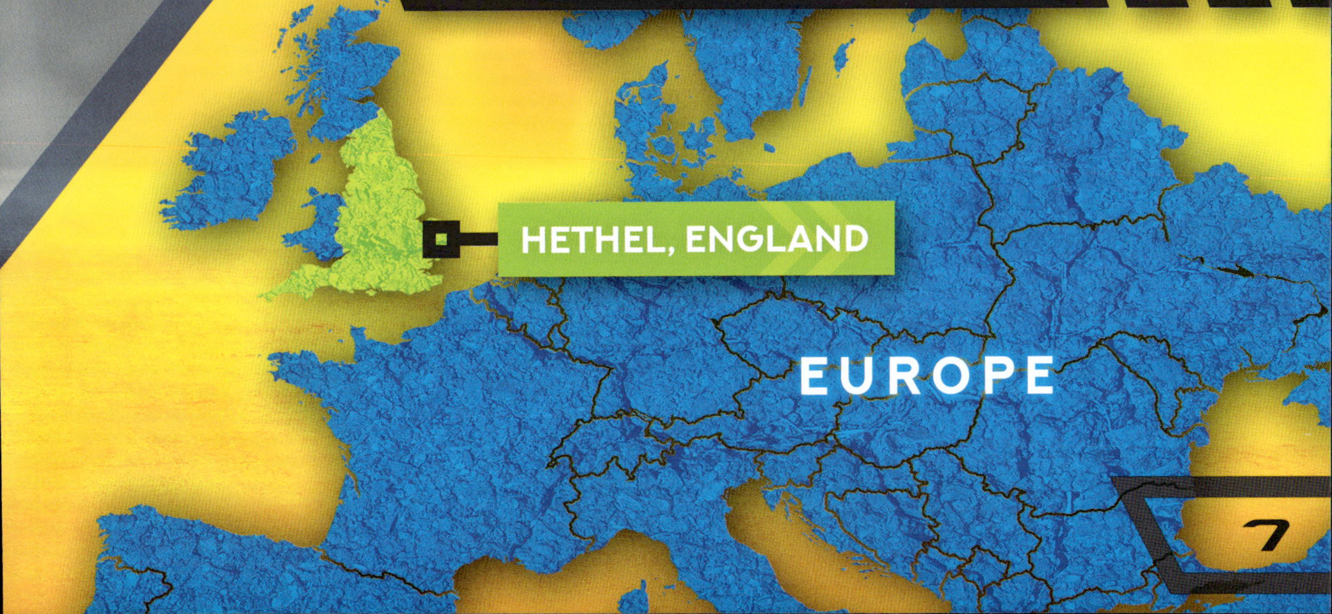

HETHEL, ENGLAND

EUROPE

7

The Lotus Evija was first shown in 2019. It is the first all-electric car in Lotus's history. The Evija is the fastest Lotus ever. It reaches top speeds of over 200 miles (322 kilometers) per hour!

EVIJA BASICS

YEAR FIRST MADE	2021
COST	starts at $2.3 million
HOW MANY MADE	130

FEATURES

laser light headlights

doors that open upward

rear wing

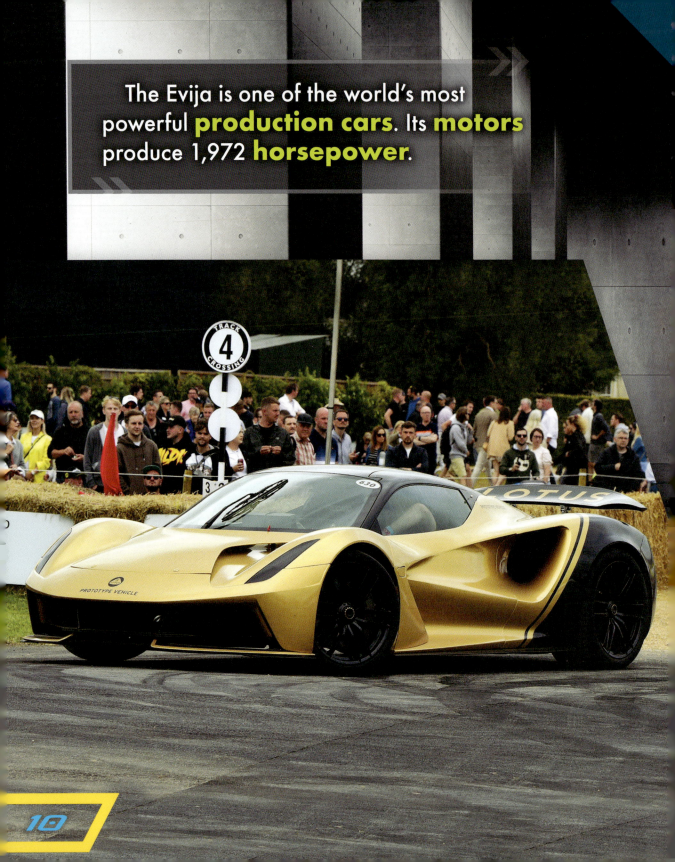

The Evija is one of the world's most powerful **production cars**. Its **motors** produce 1,972 **horsepower**.

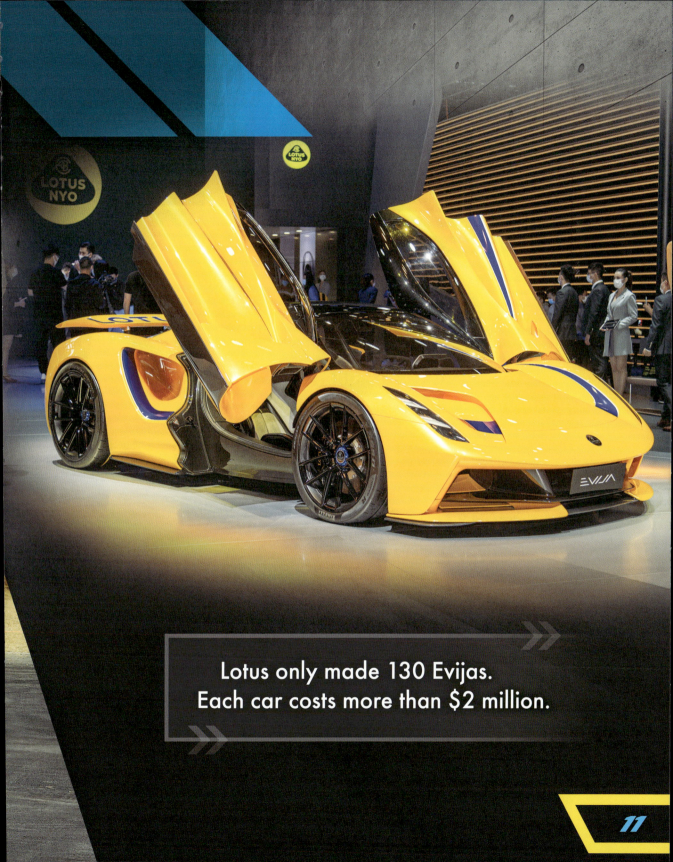

Lotus only made 130 Evijas. Each car costs more than $2 million.

PARTS OF THE EVIJA »

The Evija has four motors. They send power to each wheel. They are part of the car's electric **powertrain**.

The car speeds to 60 miles (97 kilometers) per hour in under 3 seconds!

🛠 MOTOR SPECS

FOUR ELECTRIC MOTORS »

TOP SPEED | over 200 miles (322 kilometers) per hour

0-60 TIME | under 3 seconds

HORSEPOWER | 1,972 hp

12

The Evija has a **carbon fiber** frame. Its headlights use **laser lights**. They give drivers a great view of the road.

<<< HEADLIGHT

SIZE CHART

WIDTH 78.7 inches (200 centimeters)

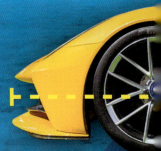

The Evija's doors open upward. These allow for easy entry.

HEIGHT 42.2 inches (112.2 centimeters)

LENGTH 175.6 inches (445.9 centimeters)

STEERING WHEEL

The inside of the Evija feels like a race car. It has a rectangle-shaped steering wheel. This is modeled after **Formula 1** cars.

Carbon fiber covers the padded seats. **Three-point seat belts** keep drivers safe.

SIDE CAMERA

CAMERAS

The Evija has no side mirrors. It has cameras on the front, roof, and sides. Outside images are shown on screens inside the car.

The Evija's **battery** charges quickly. It takes just 18 minutes to fully charge.

ALL IN A NAME
Evija means "the living one."

BATTERY CHARGING PORT

HAND BUILT IN BRITAIN BY LOTUS

The car can travel 250 miles (402 kilometers) after charging. Drivers can check battery life through an **app**.

THE EVIJA'S FUTURE >>

Lotus has stopped making the Evija. All 130 made have already sold. But Lotus plans to build only electric cars moving forward. The Evija helped change the course of Lotus's long history!

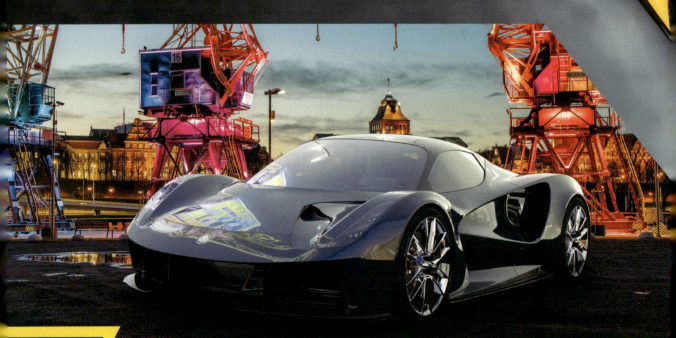

GLOSSARY

app—a program downloaded onto a mobile device

battery—a part that supplies electric energy to a car

carbon fiber—a strong, lightweight material made from woven pieces of carbon

charging station—a place where electric cars are plugged in to charge

electric car—a car that does not need gas to run

Formula 1—an international car racing series

horsepower—a measurement of the power of an engine or motor

laser lights—bright, powerful lights that use less energy than other types of light

models—specific kinds of cars

motors—machines that cause something to move

powertrain—a system in a car that delivers power to the driving wheels

production cars—cars that are made for and sold to the public

rare—not found in large numbers

three-point seat belts—Y-shaped seat belts used in race cars to hold drivers in place

TO LEARN MORE

AT THE LIBRARY

Adamson, Thomas K. *Porsche Taycan*. Minneapolis, Minn.: Bellwether Media, 2023.

Chandler, Matt. *Tech Behind Electric Cars*. North Mankato, Minn.: Capstone Press, 2020.

Murray, Julie. *Lotus Elise*. Minneapolis, Minn.: Abdo Zoom, 2020.

ON THE WEB

FACTSURFER

Factsurfer.com gives you a safe, fun way to find more information.

1. Go to www.factsurfer.com.

2. Enter "Lotus Evija" into the search box and click 🔍.

3. Select your book cover to see a list of related content.

INDEX

app, 19
basics, 9
battery, 18, 19
cameras, 17
charging station, 4
company, 6, 7, 8, 11, 20
cost, 11
doors, 15
electric car, 5, 8, 20
Formula 1, 16
frame, 14
headlights, 14
Hethel, England, 6, 7
history, 6, 8, 20
horsepower, 10
models, 7
motor specs, 12
motors, 10, 12
name, 6, 18

number, 11, 20
powertrain, 12
production cars, 10
race cars, 6, 16
seat belts, 17
seats, 17
size chart, 14–15
speed, 4, 8, 12
steering wheel, 16

The images in this book are reproduced through the courtesy of: Martyn Lucy/ Getty Images, front cover, pp. 1, 14 (width), 14-15 (length), 15; MN/ Wiki Commons, p. 3; Ron Kimball/ Kimball Stock, pp. 4, 4-5; sungsu han, 4 (charging station); GP Library Limited/ Alamy, p. 6; emirhankaramuk, pp. 6-7; Jack Skeens, pp. 8-9, 9 (headlight), 14; Liam Walker/ Wiki Commons, p. 9 (isolated); VCG/ Getty Images, pp. 9 (doors), 10-11 (right); JustAnotherCarDesigner/ Wiki Commons, pp. 9 (wing), 12-13; CJM Photography/ Alamy, pp. 10-11 (left); John Keeble/ Getty Images, p. 12; classic topcar, pp. 16, 17, 17 (side camera), 18-19 (left); Andrew Basterfield/ Wiki Commons (right); Mike Mareen, pp. 20-21 (left); Malcolm Haines/ Alamy, pp. 20-21 (right).